Scan for the audio recording of the book narration.

To my forever little brother, Omid, for all the silliness and laughter. I love you very much!

Published by Forest Breeze Publishing Inc.

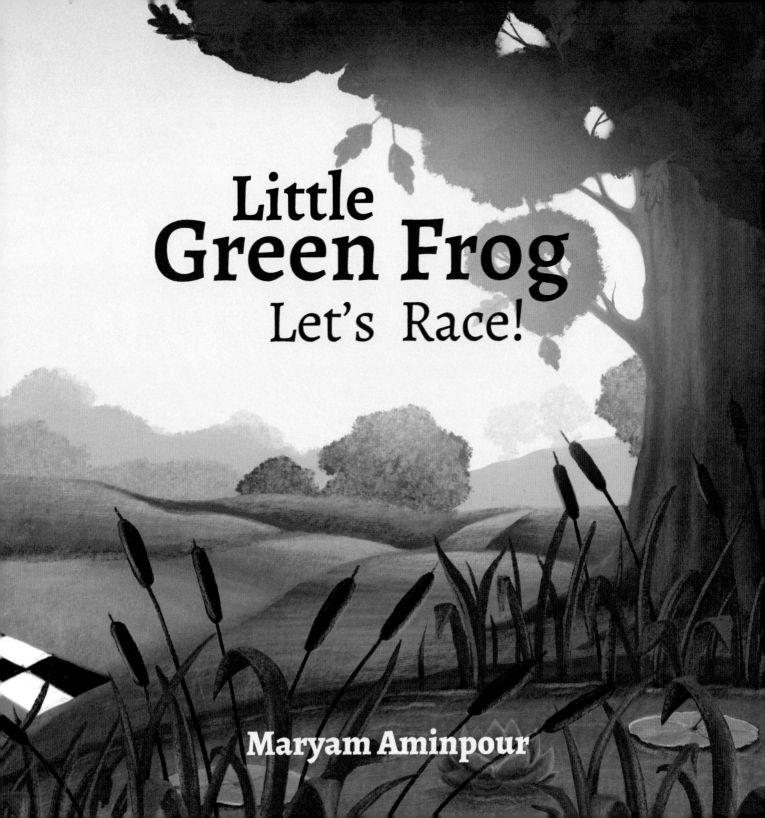

# Little Green Frog
## Let's Race!

**Maryam Aminpour**

Little Green Frog and his friends,
Want to run . . .
To where the river ends.
Whoever is first to get there,
Wins the prize . . .
A DELICIOUS pear!

Green Frog said,
"Ready? One, two . . . GO!
Hurry up, folks! Don't be slow!"

What a fast and furious race!
No one even left a trace,
Except for the Pink Snail,
Who left a mark . . .
A white trail.

Can you guess who won the race?

Here's the winner's happy face!

"Hooray! I'm first," said Blue Bird.
Squirrel is second.
Green Frog third.
Gray Alligator got there too.
He was the fourth one to get through.

Blue Bird won the prize, the pear!
From joy, he FLIPPED in the air.
They all shouted, "Congrats, Blue!
We are truly proud of you!"

Finally, it's time to go back.
But how? They have lost the track.
It's cold. It's late. It's dark too.
They have no clue what to do.

All of a sudden, they saw Pink.
She said, "I came last, I think!
But I was sure you would wait,
So we could ALL celebrate.
That's ok though . . . let's get going.
It's late! Even the moon is glowing!"

But Green sighed, "We've lost the track.
Can you help us, please, go back?"

"Of course, I will help my friends!
Home is where this white trail ends.
This white trail is made of slime,
That helps snails crawl and climb.
Follow me. I will lead the way,"
Said Pink Snail, crawling away.

An hour went by and SURPRISE!
They all gasped with wide-open eyes.
Home sweet home!
They made it back . . .
Right at the start of the track!

"Pink, this pear should go to you.
You're the REAL winner," said Blue.
"You were the slowest. You knew . . .
But that did not stop you!"

Pink blushed and said, "First or last,
Let's celebrate; the past is past."
They gave Pink a BIG SQUEEZE,
She said, "Watch my eyeballs, please!"

Green and his friends are very tired,
They go to bed, feeling inspired.

Don't EVER give up.

Try your BEST!

You CAN do it.
You'll be impressed . . .

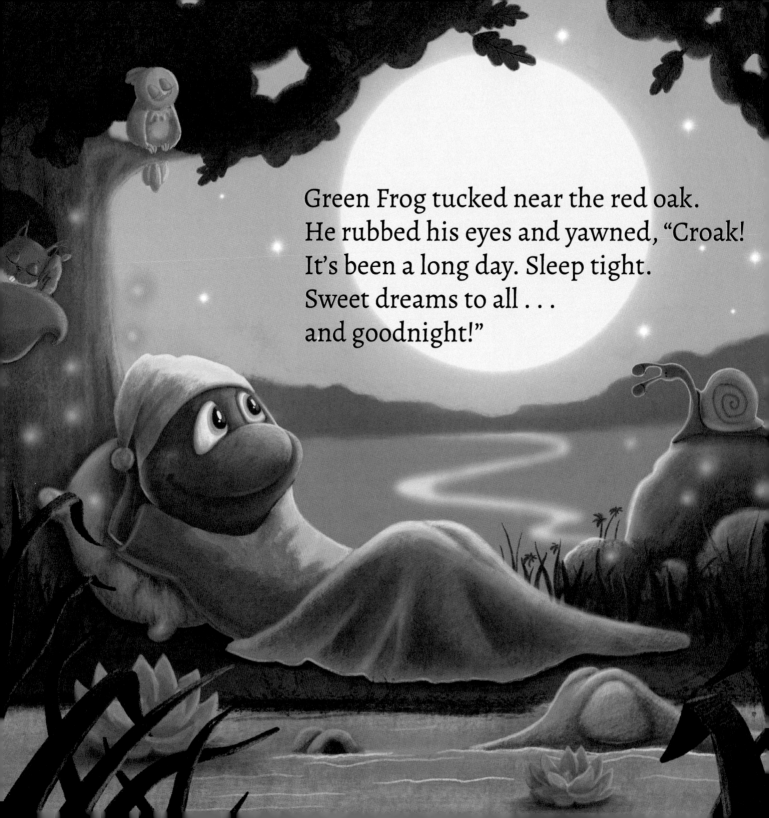

Green Frog tucked near the red oak.
He rubbed his eyes and yawned, "Croak!
It's been a long day. Sleep tight.
Sweet dreams to all . . .
and goodnight!"

Dear Reader,

I hope you and your little one enjoyed reading my book and I'm so grateful that you took the time to do so.

If you and your child enjoyed the book, please consider leaving a review so other parents could learn about my book as well. Even a short review can make a big difference and it means the world to me as an author.

Thank you!

# Look for the companion book:

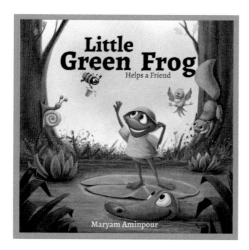

Little Green Frog Helps a Friend
Part of the "Little Green Frog" series

Made in the USA
Las Vegas, NV
12 August 2024